That's What I Call Commuting

Real Stories from Conductors on Chicago's Metra Lines

By

Ed Gabrielse and Mike Holinka

© 2003 by Ed Gabrielse and Mike Holinka. All rights reserved.

No part of this book may be reproduced, stored in a retrieval system, or transmitted by any means, electronic, mechanical, photocopying, recording, or otherwise, without written permission from the author.

ISBN: 1-4107-9709-0 (e-book)
ISBN: 1-4107-9708-2 (Paperback)
ISBN: 1-4107-9707-4 (Dust Jacket)

Library of Congress Control Number: 2003096488

This book is printed on acid free paper.

Printed in the United States of America
Bloomington, IN

1stBooks - rev. 10/04/03

Table of Contents

	Page
Introduction	vii
A New Friend	1
Blind Rules	5
The Chiseling Game	9
Parental Controls	13
My First Train Accident	17
Budget Crunch in Franklin Park	21
Handling Endowments	25
New Shoes	27
Whiggy	31
Closure	35
The Little Blue Blanket	39
To Protect and Serve	43
Dirty Ticket	47

Undies Optional	51
Bull Market Johnny	55
Metamorphosis	59
Coaches for Rent	63
Inside Out	65
A Ride on the Wild Side	67
Foggy	73
The Marathon Runner	77
Smells	81
A Free Ride	83
The Best Train Wreck of All	87
The Pacifist Trainman	91
The Chiseler	95
Lucky Once	99
A Father's Revenge	103
The Case of the Swerving Train	107
Green River	111
Home for Christmas	115
A Sporting Event	121
Phosphorus	123
Loss of Control	127
Disruption	131
Bouncing Briefcase	135
College Avenue Willy	139
Kids	143

That Day 145
Opie 149
Appendix 155

Introduction

What follows is a collection of about 40 incidents that have occurred on Chicago's commuter lines.

Some of them will make you laugh. Others will bring tears to your eyes.

Every one of the stories is true although the names, dates and Metra lines have been scrambled. Veteran riders will be able to identify many of these stories.

Mike has worked on the railroad for almost 30 years. He would like to say that he has seen it all. But every week something happens that seems to come out of left field.

Conductors and trainmen are the part of the crew that most passengers see and interact with. Because they are always there, passengers do not pay much attention to the crew. It seems like they are simply part of the train. This gives the train crew a unique opportunity to observe people with few inhibitions.

Ed is a veteran Metra passenger. He recalls many of these incidents personally. He has been bombarded with flying fingernails, falling cups of coffee and suffered through the irritation of newspapers ruffling his hair as he has tried to take a nap on the way home.

There are thousands of Metra stories that deserve to be documented – and more are being created every day.

As you experience incidents that you think should be in our next book, we invite you to visit http://www.thatswhaticallcommuting.com and jot down a few of the specifics. You can also order copies of the book for family members and friends.

We hope you really enjoy this collection, after all, that is the reason for this book.

Regards,
Mike Holinka Ed Gabrielse

A New Friend

Every weekend train is unique because many of the people are infrequent passengers or riding the train for the first time.

Often the runs on Saturday are set-up in such a way that some of the people you bring into Chicago in the morning are the same ones you see on their way back later in the day.

At Belmont, a woman got on the train with two young boys about 7 and 9 years old. Children are always intrigued with the train and the people that work them.

In the morning, the trainman that collected the tickets from this woman and the two boys exchanged several cordial comments. He explained what the pattern of two long, one short and one long blast on the whistle meant.

Ed Gabrielse and Mike Holinka

So when they came to take the train home in the afternoon, everyone acted as though they had known each other for ever. They got on the train and took seats on the upper level – which is where most kids prefer to ride.

Everything seemed normal to everyone, except the younger of the boys. He became very quiet and was not fidgeting in his seat. His mother thought he was tired from a full day of running all over Chicago.

Actually, it had more to do with that last hot dog and how it was reacting with the caramel corn, soft pretzels and chocolate ice cream he had eaten earlier.

He sat as quietly as he could for as long as he could.

Suddenly, without warning, and at precisely at the wrong time he leaned against the railing and released the reason for his discomfort.

As luck would have it, his new friend, the trainman, was collecting tickets just below.

His aim was perfect and the timing – precise.

I don't know if you have ever noticed, but the tops of the hats worn by trainmen are not solid. Rather the tops are a porous mesh.

The stream of partly processed food and drink hit the trainman right on the top of the head and spattered nearby passengers. Several of them lost it as the rich fumes permeated the car.

The trainman's hat, rather than providing any protection actually worked like a sieve and separated the solids (on top) from the liquids that dribbled down his cheeks and under his collar.

The mess and confusion that ensued, from my vantage point with a door separating me from the commotion, was like watching a comedy routine.

I suddenly became the most industrious ticket taker that Metra has ever seen – moving, of course, in the opposite direction.

Near the end of the run, my colleague came to my end of the train – looking more than somewhat bedraggled.

"What happened to you?" I asked, trying to keep a straight face while breathing through my mouth.

And I had the chance to relive the entire experience.

Blind Rules

The rules concerning blind people on the train are quite explicit – you do not touch a blind person unless they give you permission.

Many persons try to be good Samaritans. They approach a blind person, ask them the train they want to catch and immediately grab their arm to steer them in the direction of that train. But many of them do not want any assistance.

So, after asking them what train they want to catch, the next step is to ask if they would like some help in getting there. If the answer is no, it is perfectly OK to let them go their own way.

Most blind people can maneuver through the station area as well as sighted people.

Ed Gabrielse and Mike Holinka

If a blind person answers yes, they would like some help in finding their train, you simply offer them an arm for them to grasp.

A few years ago, I was asked by a blind person to help him find his train. He was a very sprightly man of about fifty years of age. We were at the Ogilvie Transportation Center. He was running late for the 5:33 to Harvard.

I do not know how he picked me out of the crowd, but he asked if I would get him to his train as it was imperative that he catch at least a part of his daughter's school program.

I offered him my arm and we both walked briskly in the direction of his train.

He was an excellent conversationalist. We talked about the Cubs and several national political events. He really had me thinking about my responses. The more we talked, the faster we walked when suddenly, boom! His arm jerked away from mine.

I looked back and to my horror, realized that I had walked him directly into one of the pillars supporting the roof.

I caught him as he gingerly backed away from the pillar. Words cannot describe the emotions racing through my mind. It seemed all I could do was blurt out empty words of apology.

He had trusted me to get him to his train. Instead, I was responsible for his smashed glasses, the blood coming from a cut above his nose and various abrasions to his face. He was completely dazed by the surprise blow that he had suffered at my hand.

He pulled out a large blue handkerchief and wiped the blood from his nose and face. He reminded me again of how important it was that he make his train.

He assured me that there was no problem – that I should not feel badly about the incident.

Yea, right. Just then I felt like the runt of the human litter.

He said that it was far from his worst collision. He had run into many objects the size of that pillar. He thought he was in pretty good shape considering the previous crashes.

I continued to blubber apologies but he stopped me short, grabbed my arm and insisted on getting to his train.

Ed Gabrielse and Mike Holinka

Well, he made his train. There have been many times that I have had contact with this gentleman since then.

Every time he hears my voice, he zeros in on me and asks if I will take him to his train.

I guess he knows that he can trust me, but just to be safe, with a curt little smile, he never fails to remind me to watch out for the pillars.

The Chiseling Game

Over the years, we have seen hundreds of chiselers.

Most of them may get by without a ticket for a ride or two, but we catch on to their tricks quite quickly.

Of all the chiselers we have seen, one stands out in my mind as the best of the best.

He was about 18 years old. He would ride only three station stops, from Winnetka to Wilmette, four days a week, on the same train.

He looked quite distinctive. He had long blond hair, sometimes tied into a pony tail. He wore tie-dyed shirts and faded blue jeans. He obviously was atypical on a trainload of business professionals.

Ed Gabrielse and Mike Holinka

The train was an eight car set. There were two of us who worked that stretch. After two weeks, it became obvious that we had more than the usual chiseler on our hand. This guy was an expert.

It became a challenge. He would get on the train, we would close in on him from both ends. But when we met in the middle, he just was not there. He remained invisible until nearly all the passengers had detrained. Then he simply stepped off the train and disappeared into the crowd.

It was exasperating for us. We never had a chiseler elude us for so long. We decided to get serious. We would station ourselves on both ends of the train. When the guy got on, we would ask the engineer to run slow to give us extra time.

We checked the upper levels in every end of every car. We locked the bathrooms. And we purposely looked into the faces of every single passenger.

We would meet in the middle of the train with empty hands, shrug our shoulders, totally dumbfounded.

Then, when we would pull into his station, he would get off as jaunty as ever and walk away.

This intensified search went on for the next month. But the results were inevitably the same.

Then all of a sudden, he stopped riding. We never saw him again.

We still talk about that kid today. His reputation has achieved legendary proportions over time. He was the best.

We never figured out where he went. He may have been sitting right in front of us and looked so normal that we walked right by him. He may have found a secret hiding place. We just don't know.

All we know is that he was the best chiseler ever.

And if that was the ultimate achievement of his life, he has our undying respect.

Parental Controls

When the monthly tickets change over, the confusion is predictable.

Some forget to buy their new monthlies. Some buy their monthlies and in the process of discarding the old ones, destroy the new ones instead.

There are always a few individuals who attempt to take advantage of the situation. Some will hide most of an old monthly ticket in a book so they do not have to use their single ride tickets. There are very few tricks that seasoned conductors have not seen.

The most vigilant police are the veteran riders who know that cheaters will ultimately cause their ticket prices to increase. Besides, it makes them angry to see someone else get for free what they have had to pay for with their hard earned dollars.

Ed Gabrielse and Mike Holinka

On the first day, the conductors will visually fix on one or two features of the new tickets that are different from the previous month. While the images change, that is not what the conductors focus on. Rather, it is usually the name of the month and the male/female designation.

One morning, on the first day of the month, I called for tickets and reminded the riders that last month's tickets were only valid for the ride into Chicago. I began to move down the aisle to check tickets.

The first two or three seats were quite conventional. Then I came to a group of veteran riders. The month designation was right and I was about to move on when I noticed the image on the ticket. It was not a station or feature of the railroad. Rather it was a very revealing image of a woman.

I did a double take. I looked at the next ticket. It was a naked man. The women passengers had male images and the men had female images on their tickets.

My first thought was that someone at Metra was responsible. Finally, as the entire car exploded in laughter it dawned on me that the joke was on me.

This practice went on for several months and then it suddenly stopped. I later found out why.

One evening, near the end of the month, the woman who was busy assembling the risqué tickets was surprised by her 15 year old daughter. The daughter demanded to know what her mother was doing with pictures like that.

The mother tried to explain, but was totally unconvincing.

The next night, when the mother had to get all of the tickets printed, the computer would not pull up the pictures. Finally, she summoned her daughter to see what was wrong with the computer.

The daughter acknowledged that she had activated the parental controls to keep her mother from viewing obscene sites on the internet.

Nothing the mother could do would pry the password out of her daughter.

He daughter was convinced that parental controls were designed to be used for exactly that – Parental Control.

Ed Gabrielse and Mike Holinka

Since the real reason came out, there have been no more obscene tickets on my trains.

My First Train Accident

I can never forget the first time I was involved in an accident with a pedestrian.

It was early December – about 7:40 in the morning. There was a light coating of snow on the ground. All indications suggested a routine run into the city.

As we neared the West Hinsdale station, I was six cars deep in the train, talking to passengers and collecting cash fares. Suddenly, there was an unusual sound of long blasts on the whistle, then the emergency application of the brakes.

I called the engineer on the intercom and heard him say that we had hit a pedestrian.

I made my way back to where the body was lying.

The experience was surreal. My mind did strange things as I looked at what was left of a person's life. I know him – I don't think I know him. I must help him – there is nothing that can be done to help him. The twitching and steaming lump is still alive – it can't be alive with all those parts missing.

Then there came the sickening feeling that there was nothing I or anyone else could do. My legs became rubber. Helplessness, vulnerability, surging adrenalin, nausea, despair, self-incrimination.

I have been involved in over 40 such accidents and I remember every one as though it was yesterday. It never becomes any easier. It has to do with personal blame. There really is none, of course, but the subconscious won't accept that. The responsibility lies on your shoulder no matter how irrational or how hard you struggle against it.

I have two overwhelming fears. One is that the next accident will involve someone I know. I am not sure I could handle the personal issues.

The second is that the accident involves a child. I have three children myself and the mental transfer of one of them into the accident scene would be more than I could bear.

I have talked to engineers and trainmen that have had to deal with one or the other. They have seen friends get hit by their train. They have hit children and most of them substitute the faces of their own children on the victims as they reenact the accident. As often as not, they are incapacitated for weeks or months. Some never return to work.

The trauma is made so much worse by the inquest that inevitably follows. Everyone says that the reason for the inquest is to establish the exact circumstances surrounding the incident, but at a terrible emotional cost.

The lawyers for the deceased convey the idea that the only purpose the crew had in mind as they came to work in that morning was to end a person's life – all in the name of bringing out the truth.

As the process grinds on, there is a growing, sickening feeling. This is not a search for the truth at all.

Rather this is a search by lawyers for money at the expense of all the parties whose lives have already been shattered.

There are no winners – only losers learning to live with their losses.

Budget Crunch in Franklin Park

A well dressed woman boarded the 7:40 out of Chicago. She had been drinking heavily and decided that she should be taken to Schaumburg without a ticket.

After trying to coax the fare from her, the police were called and asked to meet the train at the next stop.

As we pulled into the Franklin Park station, just one police car was at the platform. (Usually, two or three officers respond.) The officer who stepped out of the car was a middle-aged black woman, more than slightly overweight. I was apprehensive.

But she was cool. She professionally walked down the aisle, found the woman, ascertained that the woman had no intention of paying and escorted the woman, quite brusquely from the train.

Ed Gabrielse and Mike Holinka

Escorted is perhaps an understatement. Actually, she dragged the woman kicking and screaming from her seat, to the vestibule, down the steps and into the squad car.

That seemed to be the end of the matter.

But there was a man standing in the vestibule, who, as the officer pulled the woman from the train, vigorously protested what he considered a show of undue force and harassment.

The officer stepped back into the train and seemed to pay little attention as the man continued to yell obscenities. She continued until she was standing at the same level as he was. She turned and looked at him.

In the sequence of events that followed, it seems the man reached into his coat, perhaps looking for something as innocent as a business card. But whenever there is a movement that an officer interprets as aggressive, all bets are off.

When the man's hand entered his coat, it was just a split second later that the man's body hit the vestibule floor.

The only thing witnesses remember seeing was the officer putting her nightstick back in its holder.

Franklin Park has found the solution to tight budgets. While most municipalities need two or three police officers to respond to calls, Franklin Park only needs one.

She may not have looked the part, but she had the situation completely under control.

She was not about to come out "on the short end of the stick."

Handling Endowments

Two young women got on the 6:31 train to Kenosha. They were dressed very nicely although they seemed a bit tipsy from some after office hours sipping.

They selected a car that happened to be occupied by men only. As soon as the train cleared the station, they removed their blouses and bras and paraded around in the car displaying their abundant endowments to any and all who might enjoy them.

After a few rounds, they went into the restroom, grabbed the toilet paper and began to "TP" the car and the passengers.

The conductor was a fairly timid soul who attempted to persuade them to put their clothes back on. They laughed and turned and asked the passengers, "Should we put them back on?" There was a loud boo. And the conductor retreated.

Next, the women took out felt tip pens. As they lean over the seated passengers, they invited each to hold and autograph their pendulous endowments.

When they had collected autographs from all the passengers, they calmly put their bras and blouses back on, straightened their clothes and exited the train as though nothing unusual had happened.

The remaining passengers picked up the remnants of the "TP" and went back to reading their papers.

New Shoes

Stations, platforms and crossings are especially dangerous during rush hours. There are many more train movements during these times and regular riders assume a nonchalant attitude because they have seen so many trains routinely come and go.

One early fall morning, in Kenilworth, a woman was hurrying as usual to get to the station, find a place to park and board the 7:03. Train 306 was nearing the station, still moving at a high rate of speed as this woman began to cross the tracks.

The engineer furiously blasted the whistle because it was evident that this woman was not aware of the train.

With the first blast of the whistle, she had no reaction. She just kept moving forward with her eyes focused on the ground.

Ed Gabrielse and Mike Holinka

He blew the whistle more frantically, long blasts and short blasts to bring her back to reality.

She finally looked up just as the train was upon her. The engineer could see the plaid skirt and silk blouse that she was wearing as she disappeared from view around the corner of the train. He set an emergency application of the brakes and saw in the rear-view mirror the woman lying on the platform.

He called the paramedics. The train crew ran to where she was lying. The paramedics and emergency vehicles arrived within minutes. They stabilized the woman and took her away in an ambulance.

As is always the case, the train crew tries to learn as much about the condition of the person at the accident scene. To our relief, she was reported to be in stable condition and would survive.

However, this story has a second part.

Several years later, I ran into this woman at a business meeting. I recognized her immediately, as a face from such a memorable event is not easily erased. I decided mentioning the incident would be impertinent, but she came up to me after the meeting.

I was wearing my uniform shirt and slacks and that prompted her to ask if I worked on the trains. I answered yes. And she asked if I was aware of the accident in Kenilworth several years ago.

I replied that not only was I aware of it, but that I was the trainman on the train that hit her.

I complimented her on the fact that she had survived and was obviously doing well.

She told me that after a great deal of physical therapy she could now use her right arm at about 85% of capacity. She would never be able to play tennis or any other sport that put stress on her right arm, but otherwise, she was doing very well.

I asked her what she was thinking of that morning that had kept her from seeing the train.

Very sheepishly, she said that the night before, she had purchased a very expensive pair of high heeled shoes and was wearing them for the first time. The walkway from one side of the tracks to the other was constructed of boards with a gap of about a half an inch between them. A small misstep and one of the heels would have broken or become scuffed – not a small matter to her that morning.

Ed Gabrielse and Mike Holinka

She was concentrating so hard on protecting her shoes that she never noticed the train – very nearly the size of a two story house – bearing down on her until it was too late.

She never even heard the whistles.

Go figure!!

Whiggy

This is the name that all of the trainmen on the Milwaukee District West Line used to describe her. She was about five foot seven, about fiftyish and thin as a rail.

She consistently wore a plum colored coat with a black collar and the most inexpensive threadbare wig imaginable.

She would ride exclusively on the midday hourly locals that made every stop. As soon as she found a seat, her arm went straight up in the air and in her hand was the money for her fare. She would buy a one-way ticket on the train and would ride only one stop.

The only word that anyone ever heard Whiggy say was the name of the next station. She would say it over and over and over until the trainman took her money and gave her a ticket and the change. She never looked at the change, just clutched it in her hand.

After the ticket was paid for, she sat motionless in her seat with her arm in the air. As we neared the next station, she would get up, walk to the door, step off the train, take two or three steps and stand motionless on the platform. She would hold her hand high in the air, still clutching the change and face the same direction as the train was moving. As the train pulled out of the station, she would just stand there. We could only guess at what happened after we left.

This routine never changed until the day that a new conductor thought she was stretching and simply set the change on the seat next to her. As we neared the station, her arm was still in the air. She got up and went to the door leaving the change on the seat.

She simply would not touch any change left on the seat.

Whiggy had another peculiarity. She refused to go through any door that someone held open for her.

One morning, a well-meaning person held the door open for her. She stamped her foot and uttered some guttural sounds, then abruptly turned and walked to the next vestibule where another well meaning person held the door for her. Again she stamped her foot and made the same guttural sounds. She ran back to the first door in utter frustration and got there just as the train was pulling out. She got off at the next station but was totally bewildered and disoriented.

We were shocked by what had happened.

The trainmen got together and swore that she would always make it off the train at her stop and there would be no more games with her change.

She rode for several more months and then disappeared forever. In reconstructing that final day, everything seemed normal. The change was placed in her upright hand. She managed the door without any help. She took the usual two or three steps out onto the platform.

The only thing that was different was that as we pulled out of the station, she stood motionless with her hand held high in the air, still clutching her change but she was facing in the opposite direction of the movement of the train.

For some reason, it seemed like she had turned her back on those of us who had welcomed her eccentricities with increasing affection.

Or maybe not.

Closure

It was a beautiful Saturday morning in September. The sun was shining bright. The birds were singing. The temperature was about 70 degrees.

We had just left the Fox Lake station to begin a set of runs that the entire crew really did not want to make. Each of us could have found a thousand things we would rather do than make another run to Chicago and back on a day like this.

As we neared Ingleside, the engineer began to blow the whistle frantically. We felt the brakes lock and the train ground to a stop about a hundred feet short of the station.

I opened the doors to see what the problem was.

There were about 8 or 10 people standing on the platform, with horrified looks on their faces.

I had taken just a few steps when they started yelling and pointing. I turned back toward the train and right next to me lay a man's shattered body. His blue jeans and white tee shirt were soaking up the blood.

Apparently, as we neared the platform the man was nonchalantly leaning against a light pole. He was gazing up into the air, not paying attention to anything going on around him. As the front of the train was nearly even with him, he turned and dove directly into the path of the train.

He was killed instantly.

As more facts came to light, we found out that this man was mentally challenged, unemployed and homeless.

About ten days after the accident, our crew was called into the suburban division offices to meet with one of the managers.

He was holding a short letter from the family of the man.

Even though they had lost a father, brother and uncle, they thought it was important to apologize to us, our passengers and those on the platform for the horrible experience that Saturday morning.

At the end of the letter, each of us had tears in our eyes.

While each fatal accident leaves an indelible psychological mark on all of us, this letter brought to the train crew a sense of closure.

The Little Blue Blanket

There was a very attractive woman – long blonde hair, precise makeup – who got on the 7:38 train at the Bartlett station. She always wore her wedding ring, a white blouse and a loose skirt with a hemline just above the knees. She carried a large purse.

She was dropped off by a man in a silver BMW. They would exchange a hug and a kiss. Then he would drive off as she got on the train.

As soon as she sat down, she would put her purse on the seat next to her and pull out a little, navy-blue blanket.

A few minutes later, at the Schaumberg stop, an equally attractive man would kiss his wife good bye, get on the train and sit down next to the blonde with a very friendly greeting.

Ed Gabrielse and Mike Holinka

She would spread the blanket over both of them. They would slouch back as each put a hand under the blanket. A smile would spread over both faces and remain there until the Western Avenue stop at 8:15.

Then the blanket would be neatly folded and put back in her purse.

That evening, at 5:17, as the train pulled out of the station, the same couple would be sitting together and out would come the blanket.

Again, the slouch and the smiles of contentment.

About 40 minutes later, the man would get off at Schaumburg. He would kiss his waiting wife and kids (I assumed) and they would drive off. The blanket would be carefully folded and stowed in the purse for the next day.

At Bartlett, the blonde would exchange a passionate kiss with the man (her husband?) who was waiting for her in the BMW, a sloppy kiss from the Great Dane in the back seat and off they would go.

This activity went on for over two years and ended abruptly about 5 years ago. We never saw either of them again – at least until about a month ago.

Out of the blue, the woman appeared. She was not being dropped off by anyone. She carried a very small purse, much too small for a blanket. And the man from Schaumburg – the one she used to exercise with – was no where in sight.

She was still pleasant enough – "Hi, How are you?"

But the wedding ring was missing. And the warm contented smile we all learned to love is probably gone forever.

To Protect and Serve

The train was supposed to stop in Hinsdale at 8:20 and arrive in Chicago at 8:42 am.

On the platform was an attractive woman – early thirties, wearing a navy suit, white blouse, red scarf – and carrying a small black case.

She looked at her watch, 8:25, 8:30 – still no train.

At 8:50, the train finally pulled into the Hinsdale station, fully 8 minutes after it was due to arrive in Chicago.

It was quite clear that her 9:00 presentation was not going to happen. She could only hope that the meeting was still going on when she finally got there.

Ed Gabrielse and Mike Holinka

She was the first one off the train.

A sprint to the escalators, up the second set of escalators and out to the side walk.

She waved wildly at a cab driving by.

He stopped.

She climbed in, gave him the address, and waved a $10 bill in his direction.

Much to her exasperation, the driver burst into laughter.

The poor woman, under even more stress, demanded to know what was wrong.

He turned around and she found herself looking into the eyes of one of Chicago's finest.

The officer had stopped to help what he thought was a woman in distress.

When the officer said that he could not take her there, she demanded that he hail another cab for her.

Rather than argue with her, he called one over.

She piled into the cab and sped away – leaving the officer on the curb laughing heartily and slowly shaking his head.

Dirty Ticket

It was the 10:05 out of Geneva on the UP West line. As we started our run to Chicago, I walked down the aisle of the first car collecting tickets.

I stopped by a rather strange looking man. He had a hunted look in his eyes, wore a dirty sweatshirt and his jeans had a tear near the front pocket. It was apparent that he had not washed his hair in a week or two. His face had not seen a razor in about the same amount of time.

I thought I might have trouble getting a ticket from him, but was surprised when he simply reached in his pocket and produced a dirty, but valid ticket.

A few stops later, the other trainman was collecting the tickets of new passengers in the same car. He stopped by the strange looking man who had put the punched ticket back in his pocket and asked to see his ticket. The trainman looked at the ticket, decided that it was no good, and insisted on another ticket or he would have to get off the train.

The passenger protested that another conductor had already punched the ticket. But rather than argue further, he reached in his pocket and produced another ticket.

The trainman told the passenger that he did not appreciate being jerked around by someone trying to get by on a used ticket.

The passenger apologized in a soft voice and explained that he did not want any trouble.

We were just a few miles outside of the Chicago Station when we got a call to stop the train at Kedzie and wait for our special agents (Railroad Police) to board the train.

As we came to a stop, the agents bounded up the steps and went directly to this passenger. They stood him up, marched him off the train and out onto the platform. They leaned him up against the train and began to frisk him.

The search produced a large wad of cash and from his jean pocket, a loaded .25 caliber automatic pistol.

The agents cuffed him and took him to a waiting squad car.

We later found out that this man had robbed a gas station in a town close to Geneva. After the robbery, he had run down the street for a few blocks, hailed a cab and asked to go to the train station.

On the way, he told the cabbie that he had robbed the gas station with the gun he had in his pocket and to keep driving straight to the station. The robber got there just in time to buy two tickets and get on our train.

The only person who knew what had happened was the cabbie. As the train pulled out of the station, he went straight to the pay telephones and called the police.

The trainman who had insisted on a second ticket had very little to say. But there was a perceptible wobble in his knees as the agents led the robber to the squad car.

Undies Optional

Some women get a kick out of showing their breasts. In the summer these women will get on the train with their blouses or dresses buttoned up to their neck. They will sit in the seats on the main floor.

As we come around to collect tickets, the same blouses just happen to come unbuttoned to their navels. Obviously, they have nothing on underneath.

These women constantly shift in their seats – especially as we approach a station where men are getting on or off.

Of course, as we get close to their final destination, the blouses or dresses magically are again buttoned up to the neck.

Ed Gabrielse and Mike Holinka

Other women think that not wearing panties is cool. This practice has been going on since I started on the train.

When I first started working on passenger trains, some of the "old heads" told me to be careful when collecting tickets during the summer months. Some women have a tendency to leave their panties at home and they like to watch your reaction as you find out.

At first, I thought it was just a joke that experienced trainmen pulled on new employees.

Boy, was I wrong! On my first day, I encountered two flashers on the first train.

These exhibitionists like to ride on the upper deck with their feet propped up on the modesty panel so that when we come around to collect tickets, they can hold the ticket in a position where it is impossible to avoid a full view of their privates.

Participants in this game are of all ages and all ethnicities. But one thing they have in common is that they cannot stand being ignored.

When they are ignored, the exhibitionist will go to even greater lengths the next day. Her preparations are nearly impossible to miss.

Inevitably, she will wear bright colors, a very short skirt or a plunging neckline. From the time she boards the train, you know the show is in progress.

Now comes the most difficult test for the Conductor or Trainman. Can he collect the tickets as though everything is normal?

In all of my years of witnessing this phenomenon, if you can get past the second show without acknowledging it in any way, the exhibitionist will give up.

One woman, however, broke the rule and was quite persistent. On her fourth try, she asked the Trainman, "Don't you like what you see?"

The Trainman replied with a deadpan voice, "Sure, but I have a much better one waiting for me at home."

From that day on, the woman took a different train.

Bull Market Johnny

I never learned how he lost his leg.

But give him credit, he turned the tragedy into a golden opportunity.

He had a carpenter cut a 2"x10" board about 30 inches long. At the top, it was cut into a graceful "U" shape that tapered down to about 2"x2" with a round rubber tip at the end – just like a table leg. Near the top of each branch of the "U", were slots through which he ran an old belt to stabilize the stump.

Every day that stocks traded, Johnny was on the platform at Arlington Heights waiting for the 5:23. Later that morning, at about 10:30 he was on the train going back home.

Johnny's job was that of a "Good Luck" icon to the traders on the exchanges. Those who dropped a bill into his cup just knew Lady Luck would be on their side all day long.

Many even dropped a five spot – just to be sure.

Johnny would never stand still on the bridge. It was a huge effort to walk in the sling-shot prosthesis – and he was a master at making it appear to be infinitely more difficult than it actually was.

When traders reached in their pockets and came up empty, Johnny would point out the cash machine down the block so they could get money to drop into his cup and be covered for the day. That was better than having the market blow up their positions.

Every trader could tell you stories of what had happened to friends of theirs who had ignored Johnny for even a day.

It was hard work for Johnny to get ready for work. Friday afternoon was the only time he would shave because on Saturday he had to begin growing the stubble for Monday morning.

He was meticulous in caring for his home-made prosthesis. As soon as he got to his car, he put on the medical version to avoid undue wear.

He was just as careful with his work clothes – the old trench coat, the MIA-POW sweatshirt and the one leg jeans. These were all suitably odorized and wrinkled as though they had spent the nite in the local SRO.

Johnny was one of the best.

We figured that Johnny grossed in excess of $500 a day – well over a hundred thousand a year. And it is doubtful that any of it was claimed as taxable income.

We all hope that he saved a good portion of it because in 2000, with the market going into the tank, Johnny just disappeared. Rumor has it that he got himself a cabin on a peaceful lake somewhere with a one leg fishing boat.

From his friends on the train who had to endure those mornings after he wrapped a rotten onion in his trench coat over nite, and the hundreds of traders whose success he helped to ensure year after year – Good Luck, Johnny.

Metamorphosis

Evening trains that leave Chicago after 8:00 are always full of surprises.

Many of the sophisticated men and women that wear business suits during the week change character completely after attending social functions such as the mandatory office party.

When they ride their normal trains during the week, they are remote, aloof and intense. They never miss their regular train and seem completely in control. But the annual office party never fails to take them off stride.

Of the hundreds of such individuals, the one I remember best was a gentleman in his early 50's who rode my train regularly for several years. He dressed perfectly – thousand dollar suits, beautifully knotted ties and matching silk kerchief peeking out of his breast pocket.

He had a very snobbish attitude. When I said, "Thank you" as he showed me his ticket, his look was enough to wither a mature oak tree. His message was clear – I will not be bothered by a person of lesser status.

This person stands out so clearly in my mind because I got a kick out of saying "Thank you!" to Mr. Perfection every day – and he never failed to reward me with his withering look.

One Friday nite in December, Mr. Perfection appeared to have made a little too merry in the alcohol department. That is an understatement. He was totally, falling down, smashingly drunk.

He was still wearing his thousand dollar suit, but his tie was askew. He tried to give me his withering look, but the only thing that would wither an oak tonite was his breath. Alcohol was clearly dictating policy.

It took many more steps than it should have for him to reach the train and you could see in his eyes that he was very pleased with himself that he had gotten that far.

He hesitated near the door, obviously practicing mentally what he was going to do next. As he was contemplating the navigation of the first step, a look of distress rearranged his face as something inside of him clicked and surged.

His stomach began to churn and the ultimate expeller syndrome took over. He tried in vain to hold it back, but Mother Nature was not to be cheated. She wreaked her vengeance on his suit, his shirt, his pants and his silk tie.

That meant we could not allow him to ride the train. Nausea is highly contagious. Even the slightest whiff will cause an epidemic to sweep throughout a train car.

We left him in the station for a couple of hours to clean up and to sober up.

A few days later, he appeared in his usual seat on the morning train, again, in complete control. As I approached him for his ticket, I had just a hint of a knowing smile on my face.

When he saw me, his face twisted into a look that once again would have withered an oak.

Ed Gabrielse and Mike Holinka

This time my cheerful "Thank you!" had more than the usual injection – of pure pity.

Coaches for Rent

During the 70's, most evening trains concentrated passengers in the last two cars to make the collection of tickets much easier. Again and again, the trainmen were asked about the availability of the unoccupied cars for private activity.

The couple would offer cash in a Chicago-handshake. If the conductor hesitated, the other half of the couple would extend another hand. The hesitation was simply seen as a suggestion to improve the offer.

The price that ultimately prevailed was $35.00.

What started off as a favor to one or two couples quickly turned into a secondary source of income for the train crew.

Many nights there would be 6 or 8 couples using the facilities. The crew had to keep track of the couples so they could notify them in time to straighten up and get off the train at their regular stop.

The clients were not just young people. Many of them were dressed in business suits. It was not unusual to see blue jeans, tee shirts, evening gowns and tuxedoes. They seemed to come from all walks of life.

The crew could easily make $200 – $250 each nite. For a couple of years, trainmen were driving new cars, going on expensive vacations and enjoying some of the finer things in life.

As you might guess, the practice came to an end by itself because of greed. As the price went up, the demand collapsed.

Many other train crews attempted to start this venture on their trains, but most out-priced the market.

Soon, no one was requesting access to the vacant cars.

Inside Out

There was a young woman who rode the train from Fox Lake. She was quite focused on her job. While most woman are concerned about both their job and their appearance, she was only interested in her job.

One morning she got on the train wearing a pretty, dark colored, floral dress. She immediately got out her laptop and began pounding away.

At the next stop, another woman got on, noticed that something was wrong, tapped her on the shoulder and mentioned that she had her dress on backwards.

She stopped typing for a moment, looked down at the front of her dress and acknowledged that, yes, her dress was on backwards. She could tell because the zipper that should have been in back, was in fact, in the front.

She finished working on the project and then begrudgingly went to the bathroom to remedy the problem.

When she returned, the zipper was indeed in the back. She sat down and immediately began working on another project.

Again, the other woman tapped her on the shoulder and immediately burst into laughter. In her haste to get back to work, she had put the dress on inside out.

She was so annoyed at being bothered by something so immaterial that she decided to leave the dress as it was and went back to her work.

Apparently, she wore it that way for the entire day.

I know, because when she returned in the evening for the ride home, I could not suppress my laughter – her dress was still inside out.

A Ride on the Wild Side

He was a well dressed man who was a bit late to catch his morning train to Chicago. He arrived at the station just as his train was leaving.

He checked the schedule. The next train did not stop at his station. And the next one would be about an hour later. That train was a local that made all the stops so at best he would arrive at the office an hour and a half later than normal. He thought about the three appointments he would be missing with a feeling of dismay.

Suddenly he had a very resourceful idea. There was a slow moving freight train on the second track. He could hop on board, get off at the next station upstream and catch the express – the one that would blast through his station – and arrive downtown just a few minutes late. With a surge of adrenalin, he jumped onto the nearest car.

Ed Gabrielse and Mike Holinka

As soon as the man got on the flat car of the freight train, the engineer got the signal to proceed at normal speed. As the train passed the station where he planned to get off, it was moving way too fast to even think of jumping.

It was a fall morning. The temperature was about 35 degrees and the sun was shining. The pin-striped suit and the navy trench coat (without the liner) had seemed quite appropriate for the simple commute to Chicago. But as the speed of the train began to increase the clothing proved totally inadequate.

The freight train he had chosen was primarily made up of trailers carrying mail to the West Coast. That meant this was the "hottest" train on the east-west line. Every effort was made to keep this train moving at the maximum authorized speed.

This train would run most of the trip between 60 and 70 miles an hour. That speed, if not the reason for it, became painfully obvious as the train passed his intended station and shortly thereafter, the last of the commuter stations. Any hope of getting off the train faded and for the next three hours he experienced such intense pain from the cold wind as he huddled in a heap, desperately praying that the train would get wherever it was going and stop so he could get off.

After the train rumbled over the Mississippi River bridge, it began to slow considerably. Here was the place where the next crew would take over.

The man had enough presence of mind to realize that the train was now moving slowly enough that he could get off. But he did not factor in the effect of the cold on his legs. So as he let go of the train, his legs gave out and he tumbled head over heels on the rocks and gravel of the track bed. He lost a shoe. His suit was shredded. And he was bleeding from dozens of cuts and abrasions.

That is how the police in Clinton, Iowa found him a few minutes later. They had been waiting for him to get off after receiving reports from passing trains that there was a vagrant on one of the cars. The looks of this guy confirmed their impression. They arrested the man and put him in jail.

He kept trying to tell his story to the officers. But with each telling, his story sounded more bizarre and unbelievable. He finally convinced them to let him make a phone call to his wife.

But she was even more skeptical than the officers. No one she knew would ever do something that stupid! Her level headed, easy-going, never-take-a-chance husband was clearly not the person she was talking to. She hung up on him.

Ed Gabrielse and Mike Holinka

The dejected man returned to his cell.

A few minutes later, however, his wife called back. She had called his office and discovered that he had not been to work. However, one of his co-workers had seen him walking from the parking lot as the train left the station.

They called the man to the phone and his wife was finally convinced that the man, in fact, was her husband.

Now, she had to find out where Clinton, Iowa was. He had driven their only car to work, the kids were coming home from school in another hour, and they had a parent/teacher meeting that evening. A trip to Iowa was clearly not in her plans.

But around 5:00, she was in the car headed across the state. I only wish that I had been there to witness the reunion.

Over the next several weeks, this story grew richer with each telling.

One morning in the vestibule of an inbound train, a banker was telling the story to a few of his friends. They laughed at the poor guy's misfortunes and tried to guess the reaction of their wives to such a phone call.

One man, who had been quiet through out the telling of the story, finally said, "I don't think that is funny at all."

The banker looked at him with a perplexed look on his face. Finally, the look changed to one of understanding. Softly, he said, "It was you, wasn't it?"

The man slowly nodded.

And the public address system announced our arrival in Chicago.

Foggy

It was about 7:50 one foggy night in early December. There was about a foot of snow on the ground and the temperature had warmed enough so that there was a pea-soup fog hugging the ground.

We had just pulled out of Libertyville on our way to the Round Lake Beach station. We were close to our operating speed of 65 miles per hours.

For an instant, the engineer thought he caught a glimpse of what looked like an automobile, but knew we were a couple of hundred yards from the nearest road.

When we felt the impact, he stopped the train immediately. I went back to see what had happened. After walking for what seemed like miles, (you really lose your perspective when the fog is this thick) I came to the larger part of a car body sitting on the track next to ours. Much of the sheet metal on the driver's side had been removed by the impact with our train.

I looked inside the car. There was no one there. I began to search the ditches when I was startled by a man's voice. He was calling to see if anyone was there.

I followed his voice and found a man standing near the top of a steep embankment about thirty feet from the car wreck.

I asked him if this was his car and he said yes. I asked if there was anyone else in the car and he responded no, that he had been alone.

As I came closer, I could tell that he had been drinking. He was having trouble standing up in the snow. I asked him what had happened.

He said "I don't know, but if you are the guys that messed up my car, you are going to pay."

"Your car was just hit by a train." I told him. He wondered how that could have happened.

He said that he had left a bar after a couple of hours and was driving home in the fog. He came to a section of the road that looked like it veered to the left.

It became kind of rough and bumpy, but not too bad. Then his car got stuck. He tried to get it out of the snow, but nothing seemed to work.

Then he got out of the car to see if he could flag down some help.

That decision was probably the luckiest move he had ever made. Just a few seconds after he got out of the car, it was totally demolished by our train.

He continued to fume about his car until he heard that we were going to call the police and a tow truck.

We immediately shut down all train movements through the area. Getting the police and then the tow truck to the scene in the dense fog was a bit of a trick, especially when we were not even sure of how to direct them. It took nearly an hour.

After the police determined exactly who the driver was and what had happened, they got the car onto a wrecker and hauled it away. They also hauled the driver, a man they had seen before, to the local jail.

Ed Gabrielse and Mike Holinka

The total delay for more than a hundred passengers was two and a half hours. But the end result was a very happy one. For although the people that rode the train were very late getting home that nite, there had been no loss of life.

The Marathon Runner

Since passenger trains use the same tracks as freight trains, it is not unusual to receive a call from an approaching freighter to protect the pedestrian crossing as he moves through.

That is what happened on a mid-July morning. The conductor and I positioned ourselves on either side of the crosswalk as a 90 car freight train approached the station at about 30 miles per hour.

The conductor told the three stranded individuals that the commuter train would wait for the freight train to clear the station before leaving. They all seemed to understand.

When the train was about 200 feet away, a woman with flaming red hair, wearing an off-white business suit, bolted straight across the tracks toward my side.

She just cleared the track as the engine came barreling through with his whistle blasting non-stop.

I spoke to the woman in a tone best characterized by anger – tinged with fear.

"You are one of the stupidest people I have ever seen."

"The conductor told you to wait. You not only scared the hell out of me and the engineer on the freight train, but you risked your life for nothing."

With a smile, she looked at me and said, *"No problem, I am a marathon runner."*

It was clear that she was only thinking about herself. She never gave a thought about those who watch in horror as a human body is turned into a quivering mass of raw meat.

If one board had been loose, if a strap on her shoe had broken, if the hem of her suit pants had caught on her shoe, if she had misjudged the speed of the train, if…, if…, or if…

If one of the "ifs" had occurred, her tombstone would have read, *"Small problem, but I was a marathon runner."*

Unless they are respected, trains are equal opportunity death machines.

Trains don't play fair. A 100 pound woman against a 100,000,000 pound train is not fair.

And trains win all ties.

Smells

Summer is, by far, the most interesting season for smells. These smells permeate every car, of every train, every day.

We all have coping mechanisms to get used to smells, but the conductor does not have that luxury. As he moves from car to car, his nostrils are assaulted again and again.

One particular person on the Milwaukee West line comes immediately to mind when discussing smells.

She definitely had not taken a bath at any time in recent memory. She was dressed in rawhide leather – everything rawhide – with a heavy scent of horses.

When she was on the train, you knew it long before you saw her. The smell of rawhide, horses, and well ripened body odor produced a pungent sensory overload.

Without saying a word, she had the ability to empty an entire half of a train car.

Each day, after the fare was collected, she fixed her lunch. She would unpack several slices of bread with hands that had not seen soap in a month. Next, she would unwind the cover of a tin of sardines. She would pick up several of the sardines with her fingers and place them on the bread. Next she would fold the bread over into a sandwich and lick her fingers before taking the first bite.

Then, at the height of her solitary gourmet delight she would enter into an animated conversation with herself on some subject of great importance. I do not think the conversation was in English or any other known language.

But then, I never got close enough to find out.

A Free Ride

It is common to find to find people sitting on the stairs to the upper decks when the trains are running full.

In the fall of 1985, I was working a passenger train that left Chicago at 6:40 pm.

As I approached the middle of the second car, there was a man and a woman sitting on the steps. The woman had long dark hair and was wearing a short khaki skirt. She was sitting one step higher than the man.

They were engaged in a passionate embrace.

I asked for their tickets. The woman showed me her monthly pass.

The man slowly removed his hand from between the woman's legs. She had nothing on under her skirt. It was hard to miss as her "nothing on" was staring me in the face.

He fumbled in his shirt pocket for a single ride ticket and offered his ticket to me with the hand that had been buried between her legs just a minute earlier.

I shook my head and told him, "That is quite all right." He thanked me, put the ticket in his pocket and went back to work.

I finished my collections and went into the vestibule as we were approaching the next station. I could not help but watch them through the window. It intrigued me that two people could be so brazen in public.

We made two more station stops and it was time for the man to get off the train. He stood up, kissed her once more and proceeded to the door.

He got off and walked briskly to a waiting car. In the car was a woman I can only assume was his wife. He kissed her warmly before they drove away.

That's What I Call Commuting
Real Stories from Conductors on Chicago's Metra Lines

At the next station, the woman got off the train and walked to a waiting car. She slid across the seat and gave the driver a warm and passionate kiss as they drove away.

For nearly six months, I refused to touch his ticket and the man got free rides. Then they both disappeared.

About five years later, I noticed both of them riding the same train.

To this day, both are riding the train. He has a bald spot on the top of his head. And her long dark hair is shorter and streaked with grey. Neither wears a wedding ring and there is no evidence that either acknowledges the other.

The Best Train Wreck of All

Often, rails run through neighborhoods which seem to have an abundance of bright eyed kids. As the distance to Chicago decreases, the population of such kids seems to increase.

One morning, a freight train, sharing the commuter tracks, had received permission to proceed, but no one had measured the height of the double stack trailer train.

Or, should I say, no one compared the height of the double stack with the height of the bridge near Chicago, which the train was to pass under.

The train almost made it. But a six inch difference was all that was needed to peel off the top of the upper trailers. It was like opening cans of sardines – slowly the tops peeled back as the train crew franticly attempted to stop the forward motion.

To their credit, the crew stopped the train by the time three or four trailers had their tops removed.

But as the tops came off, the contents spilled along both sides of the tracks. Mag wheels, hundreds of basketballs and piles and piles of bicycles in every color of the rainbow.

As our train approached the wreckage, the call came from the dispatcher to stop all movement. We stopped, of course, and this gave commuters front row seats to watch as the word went out in the neighborhood that the action was at the train tracks.

It seemed that hundreds of kids appeared almost instantly and a thousand basketballs were on their way to new homes. The train crew and a few police officers were overwhelmed by the swarms of kids choosing their new bikes and grabbing gifts for family and friends.

The best the crew could do was to separate an active commuter track from the accident scene. For the next hour, as each commuter train crawled past the wreckage, the commuters pressed up against the windows as six years olds tried to juggle four or five basketballs at a time and eight year olds tried to walk two bicycles, one in each arm, down the steep slope of the railroad bed.

Any attempt to stop the looting was futile. Fortunately, no one really tried. And no one got hurt.

By the time the afternoon trains reached the area, there were few remnants of the morning's pandemonium. Like the crumpled gift wrapping at noon on Christmas Day, all that was left were a few scraps of sheet metal from the tops of the trailers, a few deflated basketballs and some badly bent, but still shiny, new bicycles.

Since then, that railroad bed has been lowered by about four feet to allow double stack trains to pass.

Only those who were there, remember the smiles and joy of that early morning mishap as hundreds of kids enjoyed the best train wreck of all.

The Pacifist Trainman

The middle seventies was a difficult time for America. Ambiguity toward what was happening in Vietnam, distrust of our leaders and the influence of Dr. Martin Luther King caused many to question their values and pursue alternatives.

One of these alternatives was pacifism toward any and all violence.

A practitioner of such an alternative was a trainman who worked on the trains in 1975. He repeatedly stated that no matter what kind of belligerent or confrontational passengers he met, he would never respond in kind.

To his credit, he kept that pledge for about six months. We were working the night trains and many of the passengers were anything but pacifists. Many were confrontational. A few were insulting and aggressive as though they were forever looking for a fight.

The pacifist met his match one cold November night.

The passenger had had a little too much to drink. He was tired. And he was looking for a place to vent. Unfortunately, the pacifist trainman ran headlong into that human time bomb with only seconds left until detonation.

No matter what direction the conversation took, it quickly became mired in negative, disagreeable and derogatory comments. The passenger took the pacifist to a level of meekness that I never realized could be reached. And the trainman's refusal to argue only served to infuriate the passenger and goad him to even higher levels of insults.

Suddenly, the pacifist snapped. He took out a knife and held it next to the passenger's throat. Immediately, two of us began talking to the pacifist and eventually got him to give up the knife.

We convinced the passenger that the next station stop would be his last. He agreed – to the great relief of everyone.

I never saw the passenger again. Charges were never filed and the incident was not reported.

I later found out that the pacifist, in order to maintain his high degree of submissiveness, would smoke five or six joints during the day. The effect was to render him almost unaware of anything going on around him.

The pacifist recently retired after many years of productive and much more realistic relationships with passengers.

The Chiseler

Another Saturday morning. The sun was shining, temperature about 70 degrees, everyone was really enjoying themselves on this fine spring day.

At about the third station stop, one very unassuming passenger got on the train along with several families, a dozen or two professionals in casual clothes and some giggling teens intent on doing serious damage to dad's credit card.

The train made several more stops – people on, people off, people have tickets, people need tickets – a normal Saturday morning.

One of the crew members was approached by a passenger who asked where the restroom was located. She was told the location, but immediately said that she had been trying to get into it for the past twenty minutes but someone was in there.

Another passenger said that she saw a man go into the restroom near the beginning of the trip but never saw him come out.

I went and knocked on the door. There was no answer. The door was locked from the inside. It was probably just a chiseler – trying to ride without buying a ticket.

We often see them. They immediately go into the restroom when they get on. They lock the door and sit there until their station is called. As the train comes to a stop, they bolt from the restroom to the station platform and mix with the crowd.

Chiselers are usually easy to catch. Another passenger will need to use the facilities and the jig will be up. We simply knock on the door. If there is no answer, we lock the door from the outside and let the Special Agents deal with the person when we get to our final destination.

That is just what happened. But when we arrived in Chicago, the special agents were unable to arouse the person. They unlocked the door, but were unable to open it.

A man was lying unconscious on the floor with his head wedged against the door.

What we thought was just a chiseler had escalated into a case for the paramedics.

When they arrived, one of them was able to reach around the door to feel for the man's pulse. The paramedic found a pulse, but when he pulled his hand back his rubber glove was covered with blood.

Now we had a full-blown emergency on our hands.

The mechanical department was called to remove the door. They had to chisel the door hinges off so the medical team could attend to the man without moving him if possible.

As the door gave way, an even greater horror was unveiled. The front of the man was completely covered in blood – his shirt, pants and most of the wall and floor of the restroom.

The paramedics brought up the stretcher and lifted the man onto it.

As they put him on the stretcher, wounds on both sides of his neck began to spurt blood.

The man was pronounced dead about two hours later in the hospital.

We found out later that the man had recently gone through a devastating divorce. He had lost nearly everything he owned. In addition, the day before, he had lost custody of his three children. And just before boarding the train, he had said good bye to each of them for the last time.

He had tried to slash his wrists, but the edge of the knife was too dull.

So he stabbed the sharper point of the knife into the jugular vein in his neck. When he passed out, he apparently fell against the door in such a way that the twist of his head acted as a tourniquet.

All of us were stunned. What seemed to be a beautiful spring day, full of possibilities, was seen by another person as a day of hopeless desperation.

Lucky Once

I have carried many drunken passengers of all ages, both men and women. Just a few are truly unforgettable.

One man boarded the train in Chicago at 2:30pm. He had been drinking, but he did not seem to want to cause any trouble. He just wanted to sit and ride the train home.

But soon after the train left the station, he started to bother other passengers. He began yelling obscenities. And when the trainman came to collect his ticket, he refused to show his ticket.

The man was a giant. He was about six foot, ten and weighed nearly 400 pounds. By contrast, the trainman was five foot, six and weighed about 140.

Somehow, the trainman convinced the giant to get off at the next station. I picked him up on train 1268, the next run back into Chicago.

When we arrived back at Union Station, the police were waiting. They got him off the train, but then he became belligerent toward them. The police immediately got out the handcuffs, but his wrists were so thick that they had trouble closing the cuffs. They got one cuff secured, but because of his size, his arms were too far apart in the back to secure the other cuff.

While one officer held the handcuff, another grabbed his other arm to escort him to the lockup. This infuriated the giant. He brought up his arms and sent both officers tumbling down the platform. The situation was getting ugly.

Suddenly, a small woman – maybe four foot, ten and clearly under a hundred pounds came running up and slapped the giant in the face. She yelled at him to settle down.

Miraculously, the giant instantly changed. He became quiet and cooperative.

This small woman was his wife. She knew the whole story of his traumatic day. She found out that he was coming in on my train and showed up in just the nick of time.

The reason for his drunken state, she explained to the police, was that he had just been terminated from his job of 20 years. The company was downsizing and this was the only job he had ever had.

She did a lot of fast talking and by the end, we all had tears in our eyes.

The police released him into her custody. No charges were ever filed. While I have never seen either of them again, I hope he found a good job with a solid future.

After all, he was lucky – once. He found a wife who believed in him and stood by him.

A Father's Revenge

It was the 9:20 Electric out of the Randolph Street Station in the fall of 1977.

It seemed like a fairly normal night, not too many "crazies" or drunks. It was not even a Friday nite.

As we pulled out of the Riverdale station, I happened to look back from one car into the other. The brakeman was frantically waving to me to come back to his car. He had a terrible look on his face.

When I got to his car, there was a man standing over another man who was lying on the floor. The man who was standing had just hit a drunk, broke his glasses and now blood was spurting from a cut on the bridge of his nose.

"What is going on?" I yelled at the man who was standing. I recognized him as a regular on my train.

"I never cause any trouble on these trains," he said, "but last week, this creep put his hands on my nine year old daughter. I have been keeping my eyes open for him."

"At first, I only wanted to talk to him. But he was too drunk to carry on a conversation. Then all I wanted to do was to break him in pieces."

I convinced the drunk with the bleeding nose that he should get off at the next station. He readily agreed.

But the irate father insisted on getting off at the same station. He did not want to hurt the man, but rather teach him a lesson about keeping his hands off little girls.

We physically blocked him from leaving the train until two stations later.

I did not see the father for several weeks. But finally, he came up to me and thanked me for the way I handled the situation. By his own admission, he said that if he had gotten off the train with the drunk, he would probably have gone to jail for having committed a serious crime.

As for the drunk, he continued to ride for several years. But because he is normally inebriated, he never seems to remember anything that happens when he rides the train.

The Case of the Swerving Train

It was the 11:22 out of Big Timber on the Milwaukee District West Line.

As we slowed for the Bensenville station, the engineer blasted the whistle and locked the brakes. Regular riders know what that means.

The engineer said that we had hit a woman in a green dress who was walking on the right-of-way. As soon as we came to a stop, the crew spread out to find out what had happened.

There was nothing under the train and nothing behind the train. But a small group of people saw exactly what had happened.

They saw a woman in a green dress get hit by the train. Then she picked herself up, walked across the street and went to sit in her car.

Ed Gabrielse and Mike Holinka

We ran over to the car where a woman was sitting in the passenger's seat.

We motioned for her to roll down the window and asked her if the train had just struck her.

She answered yes, but assured us she would be alright.

But as she turned her head, we noticed blood slowly dripping onto the green dress.

We called the ambulance and motioned them over to the car. The paramedics decided that she would be better off in the emergency room of the hospital.

We filled out our reports, but heard nothing further.

About two months later, we were contacted for an additional statement. It seems the woman was seeking some kind of settlement for the accident.

According to her statement, it was obvious that the train had swerved at the last minute, not real far, only a couple of feet, and that is what caused her to be struck by the train.

I am not making this up, folks. That was her statement. Apparently she was not aware that trains have always run on train tracks. The tracks do not allow for lateral movement of even a few millimeters.

Needless to say, the woman had no viable claim. But as is so often the case, she saw the accident as an opportunity to cash in.

The claim never made it anywhere close to a trial.

Green River

It may not be true of any other commuter operations in the United States, but within the Chicago commuter operations, St Patrick's Day is the most feared day of the year.

The Chicago River is always dyed green and people, both young and old, test their capacity for alcohol consumption. Commuters who are never any trouble the rest of the year view St Paddy's day as their personal special challenge.

One year, the 3:40 West line left Chicago with standing room only. The second rear car had a few regular riders, but most of the passengers were between 16 and 18 years old and were so drunk, they had trouble standing up. They had clustered on the upper deck – about 25 of them and were exchanging challenges.

"Suck me" a male voice would bellow – followed by an equally drunk female voice," All right, if you eat me right here, right now."

With that, a young man stood up, unzipped his pants, and began target practice on a young woman across the upper deck. She taunted him when the stream fell short and sprayed the passengers below instead.

That is what I saw when I opened the door to begin collecting tickets.

I immediately shouted at them to sit down and straighten up.

This was met by calls of, f- you, eat s-t, go f- yourself.

The normal procedure is to notify the conductor who is in charge of the train and the rest of the crew that there is a problem. It is the conductor's job to instruct the engineer to notify the police and ask them to meet our train at the next stop.

In this case, the situation had arisen so quickly that I notified the engineer directly to have the Oak Park police meet the train and be prepared for trouble. Oak Park dispatched three squads – six officers – to the scene, but we got to the station before the police.

As we waited in the Oak Park station for the officers to arrive, the conductor asked me why we were waiting. I told him about the problem and that I had already notified the engineer to call the police. He became very indignant that I had subverted his authority and demanded that I show him where the trouble was. He was determined to give me a lesson in crowd control.

As he opened the door, the ruckus was still going on. He attempted to ask the kids, "What is the problem?"

He was greeted by a chorus of; "Butt out." "Nothing you can do to stop us." "You can't whip all of us."

As he stepped back into the vestibule where the six officers had now assembled, he told them, "Take them all." And they did.

The last to go was the lad who fell short in the target practice.

He told the police that his parents were very influential people in Du Page County and they would be real upset if any action were taken against him.

As I recall, not a single part of the young man's body touched the steps or the floor as he was escorted from the train.

Once on the platform, the police began getting names and addresses of all the young people. There was a lot of crying and saying how sorry they were that this had happened.

But the wailing fell on deaf ears.

The loudest whiner was the son of the influential parents. I don't think anyone ever called his bluff before. And now he had to deal with a whopping dose of reality.

Home for Christmas

It was Friday, December 23rd, and a little after 4:00 in the afternoon. The revelry, warm feelings and holiday spirit on the train was at a high point.

Two days before Christmas and everyone was talking about their plans for Christmas Eve and Sunday, Christmas Day.

Several groups were singing Christmas carols. Many came loaded with gifts they had received at office Christmas parties. A festive and happy atmosphere permeated every car.

We had unloaded about half of our passengers and were pulling into Glen Ellyn. "Don't eat too much." "Hope Santa remembers you this year." "See you next year." I even got a few gifts from long time friends.

Then suddenly, several long blasts on the whistle, and the jerk as the engineer set the brakes in the emergency application mode. Every crew member and some of the passengers immediately sensed that this could be trouble.

We were short of the station. Trouble at a crossing? A car too close to the track? A person crossing the tracks? Or, as we all were hoping, just a near miss.

But today it was to be the end of the celebrating – and pretty much, the end to a Merry Christmas – not only for the five or six hundred passengers, but especially for me.

I called the engineer and asked, "Everything Okay?"

There was a pause. I could not hear anything.

So I asked again, "Everything Okay?"

Then the answer, "Oh my God, Oh my God, she ran right into the side of the train. I can't believe it. Please get to her quick, see if she is all right. My God, it's Christmas. I can't believe she did that."

With my heart in my throat, I opened the door to take a look. The sun was nearly set in the cold grey sky. Up ahead I could see what looked like a body laying on the platform.

As is always the case in these situations, thoughts about the person's family and loved ones become intertwined with your own family.

As I neared the place where the person was lying, it was obvious that I could do nothing for her. Everything clicked into slow motion.

Everyone seemed to be moving and talking very, very slowly. Almost to the point that I could not understand them even though I was staring right at them. I just could not understand them and the more they said, the more indistinguishable it became.

Her personal effects were scattered all over the area. She had been carrying a pizza and parts of it seemed to be everywhere.

In less than two minutes, a doctor appeared. He had been among the passengers. He began to do whatever could be done for the woman. A few minutes later, the paramedics were on the scene, then a helicopter to take the woman to a hospital in Chicago.

The doctor said that because of the severity of the head injuries, the prognosis was not good. We found out later that she died on the way to the hospital.

The engineer was in a very bad emotional state. Between the holidays and the disaster he had just witnessed, he needed a little more time before he could continue the run.

One of the managers from the diesel engine facility decided to ride up in the engine with him to help him cope. I did not see the engineer again until we detrained in Geneva.

Then, I sat with him for a few minutes to see how he was dealing with the situation. All he could do was mumble, "That was someone's wife and mother and now they won't ever have her home for Christmas."

He was the most devastated person I think I have ever seen. He did not think that he could run the train and put the equipment away for the night. He had literally used all his strength to get the train to our last station stop.

There was no one in the immediate area that could assist us. So he sat right behind the brakeman as the train slowly backed into the train yard. After the train was safely in the yard, the brakeman sat with the engineer until he mustered enough strength for the 35 mile trip home where his wife and two kids were waiting.

He has never been the same. There is never a week that goes by without some reference to the accident.

And it has never been the same for me. Every time we pass that platform and every time I see him, in my mind I hear the phrase, "That was someone's wife and mother and now they won't ever have her home for Christmas."

A Sporting Event

In 1968, the Democrats were having their national convention in Chicago. This convention was characterized by heated political rhetoric against racial discrimination and the Vietnam war.

On the night when these clashes spilled onto the streets, there was a train on the West Line due to arrive in Chicago at 6:15pm.

It made the usual stop in Glen Elyn where two elderly white couples got on.

After buying their tickets, they motioned to the conductor and said they needed some help after they arrived in Chicago. In an accomodating way, the conductor asked what they planned to do in Chicago.

One of the men told him that they needed to know where would be the best place to go so they could "watch the riot."

The conductor was stunned. He tried to determine if these couples were for real, or if they were putting him on, or if they were completely stupid. After all, cars were being burned, stores looted, people hurt and many were being arrested.

And these two couples thought they would go into town and watch a "sporting event."

The conductor tried to talk some sense into the couples. He was successful in convincing them to take the next train back to Glen Elyn.

As he drove home that evening, it was with a sense of accomplishment. A bad situation had been averted – or at least delayed.

Phosphorus

Along the mainline tracks into Chicago, there are many warehouses. Some of them are in serious need of repairs. Often it is impossible to tell if any storage or manufacturing is being done in them.

Such was the case with a building located a few miles from the Chicago Terminal and less than a hundred feet from the tracks.

It was about 10:00 in the morning when a huge explosion rocked the neighborhood around the building. Immediately flame began shooting out of all the windows and the roof. The fire quickly escalated into an inferno with white hot temperatures. This warehouse was a storage facility for many barrels of phosphorous.

While phosphorous is quite difficult to ignite, once started it is almost impossible to extinguish. When water is applied to it, the intense heat breaks it down into hydrogen and oxygen which then explodes and burns even more intensely.

After reaching the "white hot" stage, more and specialized fire fighting equipment was brought in. All train movements were halted. By the beginning of rush hour, the fire was still burning vigorously. Most of the train cars were in the yard and could not get past the point of the fire.

By this time, hundreds of earlier commuters who had not been able to leave, were joined by the thousands of regular riders who were descending on the train station expecting a routine commute home.

Instead, they were escorted, in groups of 200 – 300, to the "L" station on Clinton Street and taken to the Oak Park station where the few trains available picked them up and took them to points West.

The mixture of people was most interesting. Children walking or in strollers, older people, blind people, deaf people, a few on crutches, many with shopping bags, some who had never taken the train to Chicago before. Some were panicky or apprehensive. But no one complained about the inconvenience. They followed every instruction to the letter.

Everyone eventually got home, some 2 or 3 hours later than expected.

The most powerful view of the fire could be seen as the "L" passed about a half a mile south. Even at that distance, the heat could be felt and the light could be seen.

By about midnight, the fire department finally had the fire under control. The next morning, after a thorough inspection of the track and signal line, the trains were allowed to pass the scene.

And what a scene it was. The telephone poles were cinders, the fence around the warehouse was a series of puddles of hardened metal. The I-beams that supported the structure were bent into grotesque shapes by the intensity of the heat.

The rubble remained for several months before clean up began. Every day as we passed the scene, it was impossible not to look out in awe at the immense damage that heat of that intensity could cause to a building.

Loss of Control

It was the 10:30 Burlington Northern headed for Aurora. These late night trains are always loaded with people from different walks of life.

One such individual was well dressed in a three piece suit, nice shoes and carrying a black leather brief case.

When he got on the train, no one would have imagined that there would be any trouble with this man. He took his seat on the upper level and quietly sat down.

Just as we were pulling into Cicero, the man began shifting in his seat and suddenly bolted towards the rest room. He had not gotten three steps when he paused, shuddered a little, unzipped his pants and began urinating on the passengers below.

Ed Gabrielse and Mike Holinka

The surprised looks on their faces turned into anger as the source of the shower that drenched their clothes, hair and newspapers became apparent.

Instinctive retaliation was on everyone's mind as they surged forward. If the looks on their faces left any doubt, their language certainly did not.

We had to move fast to avoid a potentially horrible situation. I positioned myself between the sprayer and the sprayees and told everyone to settle down. We would sort out the situation.

I pulled the sprayer into the vestibule and made it clear that he was getting off for his own safety. He whimpered that he would have a hard time getting to his stop if he had to get off so early. He complained that there was no other way he could get home.

I reminded him that there were 20 men waiting in the car who would make that the least of his worries.

Just then, the train jerked to a stop. I opened the doors, pushed him onto the platform and immediately closed the doors. Three passengers were looking through the vestibule window and saw what I did and they were not happy!

They confronted me and insisted that I reopen the doors and let them get the guy. I informed them that I had to call the police first.

That seemed to slow them down and the train began to pull away from the station.

Every station that added distance between them and the sprayer helped to calm the situation (and dry the spray).

By the time the last of the would-be assailants got off the train, they thanked me for the way the situation was handled. They were grateful that they were prevented from turning a bad situation into one that would have been much worse.

I remember the sprayer and many of the sprayees quite clearly. Apparently, he got home that night because he still rides occasionally. One day, two of the would-be assailants were riding in the seats right across the aisle from him. Another sat right behind him. Thankfully memories fade quickly – no one recognized the other.

And I had to hide a smile as I began to check the tickets.

Disruption

It was a beautiful summer afternoon in August. All train operations had been proceeding with very few problems for almost a month.

After working the trains for several years you get used to the feeling of the normal operation of the train through every mile of the track. You can feel every variation in the speed or the smallest bounce of the track.

I was the conductor on an express train traveling from Chicago with the first stop about 25 miles out. Normal operation on this stretch of smooth and straight track was about 65 mph.

The first indication of trouble was a series of long blasts of the whistle. We tensed, as the engineer threw the train into emergency brake application. I reached for the intercom and asked the engineer, "Are we Okay?"

The answer was just a whisper, "I don't think so. He was standing between the rails."

The train ground to a stop and the drill began. Out the door, on the ground, you make your way, half-heartedly, towards the rear of the train to see if there is anything that can be done for the injured person.

This time it became immediately apparent that the answer was no.

Directly in front of me, in the rocks, sat the upper torso of the victim, his arms twisted into grotesque shapes.

I called the engineer and told him to get the Commuter Operations to call the police and coroner to our location.

The task of taking names, vehicle license numbers and establishing a list for the police of those who witnessed the accident begins. If possible, we try to get some type of statement from witnesses before their observations begin to degrade. Witnesses, within the first hour of an accident, are willing to volunteer their observations. Later, they begin to have second thoughts on whether or not to get involved.

Sometimes, when collecting names, someone will step forward who knows the victim. That is just what happened this time.

The person was a 25 year old male who had been married just one month. He had no record of psychotic behavior or mannerisms.

While there were no indications of the reason, we spotted similarities to other suicides. Nearly every person, who decides to end their life under a train, acts in a very similar way just before their death.

In a suicide, the victim runs back and forth across the tracks in front of a high-speed approaching train. It is like they are trying to make up their minds if this train is the one they are going to use to end it all.

Then, it seems they make up their mind and pause between the rails looking directly at the train.

When the train is about a hundred feet away, they turn their back to the train, awaiting the final impact.

After a fatal accident, it usually takes about 2 hours before the coroner will release the train. And each train backs up the remainder of the rush hour trains.

Ed Gabrielse and Mike Holinka

Often, tens of thousands of commuters will get home too late for dinner, parent-teacher conferences, a daughter's soccer game or a class at a community college.

While that may be a serious disruption, very few commuters complain. They instinctively realize that the loss of an hour or two is not nearly as much of a disruption as the fact that there will always be an empty chair at the dinner table in a home not very far from the track.

Bouncing Briefcase

It was a Friday in the summer of 1981. I was operating an afternoon train out to Fox Lake.

As we were leaving the Morton Grove station, a woman burst into the vestibule in which I was standing.

She spilled out her story: Apparently a man had taken an aisle seat next to her. He was well dressed and quite pleasant.

As soon as we had passed through the car collecting tickets, he began fumbling with his hands under the brief case on his lap. I passed through the car again to announce the next station but did not notice anything unusual. As soon as I was gone, apparently he tipped the briefcase upright exposing himself to the woman.

Through two additional stops, he would cover up as I went through the car and as soon as I was gone, he would tip the briefcase upright again. Finally, the woman leaped over him and sprinted to the vestibule.

I immediately confronted the passenger and he denied everything. In fact he threatened to sue me and the railroad for embarrassing him in front of all the other passengers.

I went back into the vestibule. The sobbing and bewildered woman was enough to convince me who to believe.

I made a call to the engineer to have the police waiting at Northbrook.

As we slowed for the Northbrook station, apparently he spotted the police cars and made a dash into another train car. Two officers boarded the train. Two others stayed on the platform with the woman and me.

As the man stepped off the train and began running across the parking lot, the woman spotted him and alerted the police on the platform. They sprinted across the parking lot and tackled him at the last row of cars.

That's What I Call Commuting
Real Stories from Conductors on Chicago's Metra Lines

The woman identified the man and went to the police station to write up formal charges. The police took the man to the local jail.

I gave the woman my name and phone number if she needed me to testify in court, I also asked her to call me and let me know what happened.

She never called and I never learned how this incident was resolved.

College Avenue Willy

He was the late night trainman's best friend.

Willy was a graphic artist who often worked into the night. He also had been a Golden Gloves boxing champion.

He was very friendly and easy to like, especially when he was feeling good after tossing a few. Willy always stood in the vestibule because he liked the openness and not having to put up with some of the people in the cars.

Willy rode our trains form about 10 years. He was well known by the train crews for his ability to quickly resolve difficult situations.

Many evenings, Willy would watch as we escorted unruly passengers off the train. After a few weeks, he took one of us aside and suggested that if we had problems with any passengers, to simply bring them out to the vestibule and he would take care of them.

Willy was good. He would win their confidence very quickly and then move closer to the individual. When it was a good moment, he would finish the conversation with the speed of his hands and sometimes his fists.

A miraculous transformation would occur. After 10 minutes in the behavior modification suite with Willy, the passenger would be changed forever. From then on, the passenger would be cooperative and, as far as we could tell, there was never another problem with one of Willy's clients.

We would thank Willy again and again for his help. But he just shrugged it off. Instead, Willy would thank us for allowing him to practice and sharpen his unorthodox techniques.

Passengers who never needed a counseling session with Willy, were grateful for thousands of quiet, uneventful rides.

Passengers who received his services would either change their belligerent ways or find a different train to take home in the evening.

Willy, wherever you are, your friends on the West Line say thanks — and good luck.

Kids

Weekends and holidays are the hardest time to work on the trains.

Each of the crew has a family at home and the deepest desire to be with them on these special days.

One consolation is that lots of starry eyed kids often ride these trains. Not the kind that cause a commotion, but the ones that are genuinely thrilled to be riding the trains for the first time in their lives.

Every time you pass them, their mouths are open in wonder, their eyes are sparkling and they are alert to every part of the passing scenery – in the car and outside.

It is so fulfilling to spend a few extra minutes with these young friends and make this train ride really special. I suspect that my face is prominent in thousands of family scrapbooks. I know that I have taken countless pictures of children, families and even visitors from other states and countries. The act of helping them produces a warm glow in their hearts and certainly in mine.

As I move from car to car, there seems to be an endless supply of wide-eyed kids. It is fun to engage them, to ask them questions, to provide a few facts and to see how they respond.

At the end of the day, I am usually drained from the energy expended in making this trip as memorable as possible for each of these kids.

When I return home to my own kids and family it is with the sense of knowing that I have been able to share what I have learned from the love and support of my own family with hundreds of others. That is real job satisfaction.

And, I am sure that the joy and enthusiasm of hundreds of wide-eyed kids in some mystical way is transferred to my wife and kids as we celebrate our holidays and special times together.

That Day

September 11th, 2001 was the most unforgettable day of my life. It was a bright sunny day in Chicago. I had just brought in my morning train and stepped out in front of the depot to relax and watch people.

My cell phone rang. It was my wife. She said that a small, single engine plane had just crashed into one of the twin towers in New York. We commented on the fact that it was certainly unusual for a plane to have clearance to fly that low and moved on to other topics.

A few minutes later, the cell phone rang again. This time she said that a 767 had just crashed into the second tower and that the first one was a 767 as well. I looked up at the Sears Tower, just a few blocks away, and saw the contrails of several planes behind it. I remember a shiver passing through my body even though the temperature was 70 degrees.

Ed Gabrielse and Mike Holinka

I was off duty and my first thought was how to get out of Chicago and into the embrace of those I love. The next train out did not leave for a half an hour, the longest half hour of my life.

My wife kept reporting the scenes of terror – the crash into the Pentagon, the crash in the fields of Pennsylvania and the grounding of all aircraft in the country.

Finally, the train pulled out of the Chicago station. We were about 12 miles out of Chicago when the call came from Commuter Operations ordering that all trains not on scheduled runs return to the Chicago station along with all train and engine crews.

All of the people that we had just brought in, had been let off of work and were streaming toward the station. They needed us to get them out of Chicago.

With mixed emotions, we abandoned the safety and security of the train taking us home and caught the next train back to Chicago. As we approached the city, the Sears Tower was still standing, but there were no contrails in the sky.

That's What I Call Commuting
Real Stories from Conductors on Chicago's Metra Lines

The station was packed with 15,000 scared and panicky commuters. All of them knew that something terrible had happened, but no one knew exactly what, or how it would affect them and their loved ones.

Every available train was packed. The train to which I was assigned was scheduled to leave in about 15 minutes. Passengers just kept streaming in. I finally had to shut the door. We could not take any more.

Finally, we got the signal to leave. As we started moving ever so slowly, I experienced a feeling that I had not felt since my plane lifted off the ground and I was finally leaving Vietnam nearly 30 years ago.

There was a cheer as we cleared the last set of switches and began to increase speed. It seemed like hours before we reached our last station stop and put the equipment away. My cell phone had long since gone dead.

When I got home, without a word, I hugged my wife and she hugged me back. We spent most of the night contacting loved ones to make sure they were alright.

Many of the emotions we experienced that day were those we keep locked up in the innermost rooms of our minds – places we do not willingly visit.

Ed Gabrielse and Mike Holinka

On the anniversary of that day, one year later, two years later, and maybe forever, many of those emotions come alive once again. I know many close friends – macho men – who will admit to being on the verge of tears every time the subject of 9/11 comes up and even when they hear a stirring version of The Star Spangled Banner or God Bless America.

I suppose that is the way this day will always be remembered by those of us who love our freedom and our country more than life itself.

Opie

The railroad can be a difficult place to work. The long hours and days away from home can take a toll on even the best employees.

In the early nineties, the railroad was hiring about 20 people per day to take the place of those who were quitting.

One of these new hires was Joel. He was an 18 year old young man. As long as Joel could remember, he was fascinated with trains and railroading. He spent many hours watching, photographing and dreaming about trains.

When Joel was a senior in high school, he had the inevitable meeting with the career counselor. It was a waste of time. Joel knew what he wanted to do. He was born to be a railroader.

Following his graduation, he went to the employment office and applied for a job with the Chicago Northwestern Railroad. He was hired as a road freight brakeman. He could not have been happier. He knew that the railroad would eventually promote him into engine service and his life long dream would be realized.

Joel had learned many things about railroad operations prior to coming to the Northwestern, but what he did not and could not learn were the temperament, personalities and idiosyncrasies of the people working in the industry.

The Northwestern was no different from any of the other railroads in the United States. Working with the men on the railroad caused Joel to begin changing those values which he had learned at home. He found himself working with people who used alcohol, punctuated every sentence with profanity, engaged in endless moronic sexual conversations and talked in a demeaning way about women.

Joel was in transition from the blonde haired, blue-eyed, apple pie type young man to being accepted as a "rail." He wanted the job. He loved the job. And he was determined to do whatever it took to be accepted.

After about two months Joel's mannerisms had changed considerably. He was being watch closely by other "rails" to see what kind of a co-worker he was likely to become.

Apparently, they approved and as evidence, Joel was awarded his very own nickname.

Often the nicknames that commemorate this rite of passage are lost within a few weeks. But some names take on a life of their own and stick with the person the rest of their lives.

Because of his disposition, personality and naïve ways of dealing with life, Joel was given the name Opie – as in the character played by Ron Howard on Mayberry RFD.

It was 1995 when the handle, Opie, was given to him and today no one even remembers a guy called Joel.

The name has superceded the FCC rules for proper radio usage on the railroad. The typical radio transmission to any freight or passenger train goes as follows:

"Omaha dispatcher East calling Extra 8502 East, over"

Ed Gabrielse and Mike Holinka

The correct FCC response is:

"Extra 8502 East go ahead dispatcher, over"

The rules of radio transmissions are strictly enforced, especially since the Union Pacific took over the operations of the Northwestern. The UP monitors radio conversations and doles out discipline at a much greater rate than the management of the Northwestern.

But even on the UP you will hear:

"Omaha dispatcher East calling "Opie" over"

And the response comes back:

"This is "Opie", dispatcher, go ahead, over"

Not long ago, an East bound freight called the dispatcher to see what train they were waiting for and how long it would be before they could proceed. It went like this:

"Extra 8519 East at MV calling the Omaha dispatcher East, over"

"Dispatcher East, go ahead Extra 8519, over"

That's What I Call Commuting
Real Stories from Conductors on Chicago's Metra Lines

"What are we waiting for and about how long are we going to be here, over"

"You are waiting for an Opie double stack. He should be there shortly. Just a minute, I'll call and see where he is now, over"

"Omaha dispatcher East to Opie, over"

"This is Opie, go ahead dispatcher, over"

"How long until you expect to be at MV, over"

"It will be about 15 minutes, dispatcher, over"

"Thanks a lot Opie, dispatcher East, out"

"Okay, dispatcher, Opie, out"

A few weeks after Opie came on my commuter train as the engineer, we had a cranky passenger. He could not understand why the train was going so slow at a point near our final station stop.

I explained to him that "automatic train control" would kick in if we went any faster because another train was in the block ahead of us.

But he was not in any mood for a real explanation. Instead, he said, "This is the first day I took the train. It was late this morning and it is late again tonite. I cannot believe that you call this commuting."

I simply turned away. You learn very quickly to avoid arguments with passengers on issues you cannot change. I happened to mention the incident to Opie.

I do not know if the same passenger was on the train the next day. We were having a superb run time-wise. We were approaching Geneva, our final station stop about four minutes ahead of time.

Opie could not help himself. He picked up the PA and with a voice brimming with pride, announced to the entire train, "Folks we are four minutes early. Now this is what Opie calls commuting."

The entire train exploded in laughter.

Appendix

The Ten Commandments of Riding the Rails
(And Suggestions for Coping with Those who Flaunt Them)

I. Watch those passengers who, after selecting a seat, put their coffee on the seat while removing their jacket. The jacket will hit the coffee and the liquid will puddle on the seat underneath you. Instead, grab it quickly and hold it until they are seated. As they reach for it, take a small sip, smile, say thank you, and hand it back to them.

II. When an unknown person reaches across you to hang a coat on the hook on the wall, make sure that a portion of their coat contacts the floor. In the winter, the floor is covered with salty mud and slush, and in the summer with sticky pop.

III. Select a seat next to someone with a small footprint (really thin). If someone with a large footprint sits next to you, feign sleepiness and get really cuddly with them. They will find another seat as soon as possible.

IV. Look at the tickets of already seated passengers. In an outbound train, select a seat mate with a short ride (as in Zone B, or C). After they leave, you can stretch out for the rest of the trip.

V. When seats are in short supply, look for seats occupied by packages. Simply ask the person if they have a ticket for those packages. If not, go ahead and move them – assuming the owner is smaller than you.

VI. Avoid people with cell phones. Always be prepared to whip out your phone to describe in gory detail your mother-in-law's gall bladder surgery in a louder voice than they are using.

VII. Avoid the lower level if possible. Stuff falls – newspapers, umbrellas, fingernail clippings, curlers, cell phones – and some of it hurts.

VIII. Check the reading materials of the person sitting in the seat behind you. As you go to sleep, a newspaper rustling your hair is sure to bring you out of the deepest sleep.

IX. If you are sitting near the window, always get up at least two stations before your stop. It makes it much easier to put on your coat, it eases the pain in the lower back and you can join the group that is blocking the aisle.

X. Listen carefully to the excuses the conductors give for late arrivals (not the ones on the PA, but the ones they tell you personally). Their excuses are usually more creative than the ones you make up to tell your spouse.

About the Authors

Mike Holinka is a veteran Conductor of almost thirty years. Metra riders on the West Line will recognize him as the personable, unflappable arbiter of every problem.

Ed Gabrielse is a veteran passenger of nearly twenty-five years. He could be found in the first half of the second car until his recent retirement.

In this book, Mike and Ed give an inside, unvarnished view of what really flies on Metra.